Arnold for President

ISBN 0-439-23263-5

12 11 10 9 8 7 6 5 4 3 2 1   0 1 2 3 4 5/0

Printed in the U.S.A.

First Scholastic printing, September 2000

Arnold for President

by Craig Bartlett

interiors illustrated by
Tim Parsons

cover illustrated by
**Tuck Tucker, Kenji Notani,
and Teale Wang**

SCHOLASTIC INC.
New York Toronto London Auckland Sydney
Mexico City New Delhi Hong Kong

CHAPTER 1

The morning bell rang at P.S. 118. Arnold hurried to class through a hallway packed with kids. He turned a corner and skidded right into Helga. *Crash!* They both went down, books flying everywhere.

Helga was the first to get up. "Watch where you're goin', football head!"

Arnold began picking up their books. "Sorry, Helga."

Helga quickly snatched her geography

book from Arnold and turned smartly away. "Next time keep your eyes on the road. Sheesh!"

Helga stomped down the hall and around the corner, gripping her books and muttering to herself. "Arnold. What an odd-headed buffoon. What a dimwitted, dweeby little dim bulb. How I hate him! And yet . . ."

The corridor was empty now. Helga was alone. She blinked twice, and looked quickly in all directions: The coast was clear. ". . . how I love him!" She whipped open her geography book. Nestled inside was a perfectly cut out oval, handmade Arnold bust. "His tact. His subtle yet enormous vocabulary. His amazing attention to detail. I love him! Love him! Love him!"

Suddenly, Helga heard wheezy breathing behind her. She closed her book and slowly turned: It was Brainy, the weird kid who always happened to be standing there right when she had a single moment to herself. Brainy stared at Helga and breathed.

Helga socked him and slunk off to class.

Helga stomped into the classroom and flopped down at her desk just as the last bell rang. When Phoebe greeted her with a "Good morning, Helga," she turned and gave her best friend a scowl. "What's so good about it?" she asked back.

In the front of the room, Mr. Simmons yelled to be heard over the noise of kids finding seats. "It's the second week in October—you know what that means? It's time for elections! In two weeks, after our candidates have had the chance to campaign and debate the issues, we'll vote for this year's class president!"

Helga sat up—*now* she was awake. She had a secret thought: fourth grade class president! Now *that* was greatness. It was about time she showed that Rhonda Lloyd who was the real boss of the fourth grade. But she'd need some help—in fact, she'd need a lot of help.

Mr. Simmons turned to the chalkboard. "Okay, class. The first step is to nominate our candidates! Talk among yourselves and decide which students have that special quality that makes you want to nominate them."

Helga turned to Phoebe and hissed, low and sincere, "I want the job, Phoebes. You know what to do."

Phoebe nodded. "Nominating," she chimed, raising her hand. "Mr. Simmons? I nominate Helga."

Mr. Simmons wrote Helga's name on the board. "Great! Helga! Who else?"

Three desks over, Rhonda prodded

Nadine. Nadine winked at Rhonda and raised her hand. "Mr. Simmons? I nominate Rhonda."

"Wonderful!" Mr. Simmons agreed, adding Rhonda's name to the chalkboard. "Rhonda! Who else?"

Curly raised a hand. "Mr. Simmons? Can I nominate myself?" The class laughed; Curly spun around. "What's so funny about that?" he demanded.

Mr. Simmons held up a hand for quiet. "Yes, Curly, you certainly can nominate yourself." He gestured to all of them: "Each one of you has special qualities, and I personally look forward to Curly's campaign." Mr. Simmons added Curly to the list.

Meanwhile, Gerald was patiently trying to convince his best friend to throw his hat in the ring: "It'll be great, Arnold! And I can be vice president!"

Arnold was puzzled. "But why do you want to be vice president?"

Gerald waved a hand. "'Cause it's easy! The V.P. is in charge of . . . the Safety Patrol Honor Guard, or something. Freddy did it last year, and he says it's cool. I think we get to go to lots of free lunches."

Arnold thought about it: class president. It sounded like fun.

Gerald poked him. "C'mon, Arnold, let's do it! We can beat these guys."

Arnold grinned. "Okay. Let's do it!"

Gerald's hand shot up. "Mr. Simmons? I nominate Arnold!"

CHAPTER 2

At two o'clock the next afternoon, each candidate prepared to give their big campaign speech. Arnold was nervous: What if he promised something he couldn't deliver?

Rhonda looked over her 4 x 6 index cards and thought, I should have cross-referenced these!

Helga turned to Phoebe and elbowed her. "Let's get 'em, Phoebes."

Mr. Simmons stood up. "Okay, class. The

first candidate to come up to the front of the room and make their speech is—"

Curly's hand shot up. "Mr. Simmons? Lemme go first!" Instead of walking to the front of the classroom, Curly climbed on top of his desk and addressed the room. "I demand to be your president! If elected, I will endeavor to get us all new hats, and also promise to turn the school into a moose preserve!"

The class burst out laughing. "That's . . . that's wonderful, Curly," Mr. Simmons said. "Now please get down from there."

Curly sat down, grinning, and apparently satisfied. It was always hard to know what was going on behind those opaque eyeglasses of his.

Rhonda walked to the front of the classroom and stood at the podium, quite regal in contrast to the previous loony antics. "As you all know, I'm Rhonda Wellington

Lloyd," she said, and sniffed in Curly's direction. "The office of class president has actual responsibilities, and I for one intend to take them seriously."

Nadine led some polite applause as Rhonda continued: "And my campaign promise is to get some decent after-school activities going, like a cotillion."

More applause. "A cotillion. Wonderful," Sid said, smiling. Then he elbowed Stinky. "What's a cotillion?"

Stinky shrugged and elbowed Gerald. "What's a cotillion?"

"I'll tell you later," Gerald said, looking wise. Then he turned to Arnold. "What's a cotillion?"

Stinky turned back to Sid. "I reckon Rhonda's gonna win. What with her fine upbringin', she just kinda deserves it somehow."

But Helga was next. As she relieved Rhonda at the podium, she cracked, "Thanks, Princess. We'll have a 'cotillion' as soon as the rest of us plebes figure out what you're talking about."

Everyone laughed, but Helga scowled at them. "What're you laughing at, ya bunch of uneducated slobs? Try usin' a dictionary once in a while, for cryin' out loud!" The class recoiled, then laughed again and started to applaud.

Helga continued, pounding her podium for emphasis. "That's right, I'll lay my cards on the table! I'm Helga G. Pataki, and I'm running for class president. My campaign is simple: You all pretty much do what I say, anyway, so just vote for me! C'mon, you want Curly running things?"

Everyone glanced at Curly, who let out a short bark.

Helga pointed to Rhonda. "And Rhonda—Miss Wellington Stinkin' Lloyd? Next thing you know, we'll be drinkin' tea in the afternoon!"

Rhonda frowned, angrily turning away.

"And, please, don't make the mistake of voting for *Arnold*!" Helga said. Arnold's eyes widened as she continued. "I can't imagine a worse idea. I mean, come on!" She crossed her eyes, scrunched down, and said in her best doofus-Arnold imitation: "Ar-nulld the class president! Let's all be positive and grow wings and fly around the room, 'cause it's raining malted milk balls!" Helga straightened up and glared at Arnold. "Hey, Arnold! Life isn't always beautiful! Try being a little more practical!"

Mr. Simmons had to speak up over the chaos that ensued. "Thank you, Helga. That was a very passionate speech, but Arnold hasn't made his speech yet, and we're almost out of time. Arnold?"

Arnold walked up to the podium and waited for the laughter and cheers to die down. This wasn't going the way he'd hoped. He turned to Helga with a little smile. "Thanks for the introduction, Helga." Arnold turned to the class. "I just want to say that I'd really like the job of class president. I know there're plenty of responsibilities, but it's a job I really want. So . . . on election day, remember: Arnold for president!"

As Arnold took his seat amid scattered applause, Helga folded her arms and glanced at the ceiling, annoyed.

Seven minutes later she raced into the front door of her house, dashed upstairs, entered her bedroom, and slammed the door behind her. In the dim light she crossed the few steps to her closet. She opened the door, swept aside her dresses and coats, and knelt on the floor. Even in near-pitch darkness her fingers found the electric switch, and CLICK! a hundred Christmas lights suddenly twinkled, flooding the closet in a warm, cheery light.

Helga gazed lovingly at her Arnold Shrine. This one was Shrine Number Fifteen; her mom cleaned Helga's room about twice a year, and always threw them out, one by one. Rather than actually bring up the embarrassing subject of an Arnold Shrine with her mom, Helga simply rebuilt it. This Shrine was like the others in that it centered around a semirealistic bust of Arnold, but was woven out of grass, berries, and flowers. The football-shaped head was made out of reeds, and cornflowers were the ears. The hair was straw from her mom's broom. It had

taken Helga forever to find just the right shade of yellow.

Helga clasped her hands together. "Oh, Arnold! How torturous is this secret love! I desire to be class president, but how can I campaign my heart out when I know that *you* crave that same presidency?" The flower-eyed Arnold head stared back at Helga.

In Helga's heightened emotional state, the fake Arnold head almost seemed to speak to her: "I'd really like the job of class president."

"Enough!" Helga yelped. She couldn't take it any longer. Helga sank to the floor in despair. "But what about me? I'm *dyin'* to be president!"

CHAPTER 3

That night, at the Sunset Arms Boardinghouse, Gerald lay on the couch and tossed a football in the air as Arnold paced back and forth. "The debates are tomorrow. We need one really great campaign promise."

Gerald tossed the football up and caught it. "How about a three-month school year? Tear down the cafeteria?"

Arnold shook his head. "I'm serious."

"How about if we raise money to build a skateboard ramp? The kids at P.S. 119 built one in their school yard. They raised the money with bake sales and stuff." Arnold brightened.

"Yeah, we could do that!" Gerald jumped up, passing the football to Arnold. "We'll make it our campaign platform."

Arnold bobbled the pass, but grinned, anyway. "Yeah! A skateboard ramp for P.S. 118!"

A similar scene was taking place at the Pataki home: Phoebe paced in front of Helga, who lay on her bed reading a comic book. "We could . . . hand out pins with your campaign slogan on them, something that rhymes. Like: Vote for Helga, she's a swell . . . gal?"

Helga glanced up from her comic. "Better

leave the rhyming to me, Phoebes."

Phoebe nodded and turned a page in her little spiral notebook. "Have you decided on a campaign platform yet, Helga?"

Helga nodded, turning a page in her comic book. "'Tear down the cafeteria.'"

"Helga, I'm serious. The debates are tomorrow, and you need to be prepared."

Helga tossed her comic book aside. "Ahh, it'll be a snap. I'll just listen to what those lame-os have for campaign promises and then I'll tear their acts down."

CHAPTER 4

The next day, Mr. Simmons was his usual grinning self as he stood at a podium in the front of the room and explained the rules of the "great debates" to the class. "Now, let's begin," Mr. Simmons said. "I can hardly wait to hear from each of these special candidates! Rhonda, you're first! Come on up!"

Rhonda stepped up to the podium and nodded to the smattering of applause from the class.

Mr. Simmons read from an index card: "Rhonda, our first debate question is: How do you define the job of class president?"

Rhonda lifted her chin. "The job of class president involves holding weekly meetings with the class vice president, the secretary, and the treasurer. But anyone could probably do that; I intend to do more. I'm going to change the look of this classroom. Introduce a new color scheme, something less tacky than"—she gestured around the October-themed classroom—"these hideous Halloween decorations. How about something sunny for a change?"

Eugene clapped. "Gosh, that sounds wonderful!"

Helga snorted.

Mr. Simmons looked down at his index cards. "Helga? Do you have a rebuttal to Rhonda's statement?"

Helga rose and stalked to the front of the room amid hoots and cheers, then held up a hand for silence. "You want my rebuttal? Rhonda plans to redecorate this dump. I say, let her paint her *own* house purple and leave us out of it. How 'bout some reality, for cryin' out loud?"

Rhonda reddened as the class hooted.

Helga scoffed, "Rhondaloid just cares about how things *look*. She wouldn't know a class president if it bit her. I define the job of class president like this"—she poked her chest with her index finger—"me—Helga G. Pataki!"

The class cheered and applauded. Helga sat down next to Rhonda and gave her a wink. "You're goin' down hard, Princess."

"Oh, yeah?" Rhonda hissed. "This campaign isn't over yet, Helga."

"Okay, settle down," Mr. Simmons called

out. "Our next debate question is for Curly."
Curly sprang like a shot from his chair to the podium, gripping it, waiting for his question. "Curly: As president, what will you do for this class?"

Curly shouted to the rafters, "For this class? I'm glad you asked! I'll laugh and cry, spell my name out across the sky, and if that won't do, why, I'll free all the animals from the zoo!" Curly grinned an insane smile and pumped his arms in the air.

The class responded by stomping and laughing. "Free the animals! Free the animals!" Curly chanted, until the door opened and Principal Wartz stuck his head in.

"Everything all right, Mr. Simmons?"

Mr. Simmons gulped as the noise subsided. "Yes, Principal Wartz. We're just . . . at a particularly joyous part in learning about the democratic process."

Wartz looked around the room. "Democratic process, eh? Carry on." He shut the door.

Mr. Simmons turned back to Arnold. "Arnold? May we have your response to the same question?"

Arnold blinked. "What was the question again?"

Mr. Simmons smiled. "As president, what will you do for this class?"

Arnold stepped up to the podium, thinking, why do I always follow the ones who just got the biggest laugh? He glanced at Gerald, who gave him a thumbs-up.

Then Arnold spoke: "Well, I'm all for freeing the animals, but I'll leave that to the zookeepers. Meanwhile, at P.S. 118, I think we need a skateboard ramp." The kids perked up, listening. So far, so good.

Arnold continued: "The kids at P.S. 119

got one built for their playground, and I don't see why we couldn't do the same. They raised the money from bake sales, and we could do that, but why not raise the money by putting on a talent show, or a carnival?"

As the kids yelled their approval, Stinky turned to Sid. "I reckon a skateboard ramp's the one thing we need to make our recess hour pret'near perfect."

Sid nodded. "That Arnold. Why didn't I think of it?"

Harold leaned in. "Did he say something about a carnival?"

Gerald gave Arnold a thumbs-up from his seat. Arnold grinned at Gerald and gave him a thumbs-up right back.

CHAPTER 5

"Well, Arnold, our little campaign is proceeding just like we planned," Gerald said to Arnold that afternoon as they walked down the hallway toward the school's front doors, pausing to get their jackets out of their lockers. "Nice introduction of the skateboard ramp theme. But what was that about a talent show? What talent do we have?"

"We'll think of something," Arnold said. "You can play the piano. . . ."

Gerald sighed. "Everybody plays the piano at a talent show!"

Helga dictated to Phoebe as they walked down the hallway. "Find out what in the heck the football head was talkin' about. What skateboard ramp?"

Phoebe nodded, writing, *Skateboard ramp, P.S. 119*, in her little spiral notebook.

Helga continued: "We've got to dig up some dirt on the idea. Prove it's impossible, or that he's lying . . . you know, something crummy about his plan."

Phoebe looked up doubtfully at Helga. "About Arnold? He's typically quite honest, Helga."

Helga rolled her eyes. "Do I have to spell it out, Phoebe? It's his dumb, phony, football-headed honesty I'm tryin' to tear down! If I can make him look like a liar, then the presidency is ours."

Phoebe knew Helga was wrong, and wanted to say something about it, but at that moment they passed Arnold's and Gerald's lockers. Phoebe's eyes met Gerald's. There was an uncomfortable pause. "Hi, Gerald," Phoebe said in a tiny voice.

Gerald looked coolly at Phoebe, seeming to read her mind. "Hey, Phoebe."

Did he know what Helga had planned? Phoebe's heart beat faster as they walked away. Gerald watched them go, then turned to Arnold. "Phoebe looks guilty. I wonder what Helga's got up her sleeve."

CHAPTER 6

Two days later Helga stood at the podium tearing Arnold's act down while the other candidates watched, amazed, from their chairs in the front of the room. It was the second round of debates.

"Arnold knew that my dad was planning to cosponsor a skateboard ramp for the school, along with Vermicelli Towing and the Scheck Cement Company. He knew that the fifth graders were raising money for it, and

he and Gerald were pretending to make it sound like it was their idea."

Gerald jumped up from his desk, pointing at Helga. "That's a total lie, and you know it!"

The kids erupted in shouts and questions all at once: "A fifth-grade skateboard ramp?"

"Who told Helga?"

Mr. Simmons waved his arms frantically. "Class! Democracy is exciting, but please, let's quiet down!"

But Arnold and Gerald were still standing. "We didn't know about your dad's plan, Helga, because you only came up with it last night!" Arnold yelled.

Helga snapped right back, "My dad's been planning this for months. It's all on the up-and-up. You just stole the idea, football head."

There were more shouts from the class. Desperate, Mr. Simmons took a gavel out of his desk and pounded the desktop several times: "Everyone! Sit down! That's enough!" he yelled, surprising even himself.

The kids immediately stopped shouting and sat down. "Thank you." He sighed.

Arnold walked to his desk. He turned to look behind him. In the back of the room, Helga looked back at him, annoyed. "What?" she asked.

Arnold gave Helga a look he almost never used on anyone: a cool-as-ice stare. He stared at her for a long moment, then turned back to his books.

Helga felt a chill pass through her. Arnold was actually mad! Really, really mad! Over the years she had let her beloved down plenty of times—she'd had to! How else could she keep up the facade that she hated him? She opened her geography book and snuck a peek inside: The handmade Arnold bust seemed to gaze back at her in icy judgment. Helga slammed the book shut and gulped. She looked at the back of Arnold's head.

"Oh, Arnold," she breathed, barely a whisper. "I've always loved you. And I've always pretended to hate you. It's been our little routine. But you always seemed to forgive me." And just then, in that moment, Helga deeply regretted everything she had said in the campaign.

But by the time the three o'clock bell rang, Helga had convinced herself that it was worth it. She had to. How else could she stomp out of the classroom like she did every afternoon at three o'clock as Helga G. Pataki, the toughest kid in the fourth grade?

CHAPTER 7

ARNOLD IS A BIG, FAT LIAR!

It was morning. Arnold looked up at the block-lettered poster from all the way down the hall. But there wasn't just one poster; there were several. And there were many variations: WOULD YOU WANT A PHONY FOOTBALL HEAD FOR PRESIDENT?, SKATEBOARD RAMP?? YEAH SURE., and CRIMINEY! WHAT A LYING DWEEB.

Gerald shook his head in amazement.

"Mmm, mmm, mmm. Arnold, we have *got* to counterattack."

Arnold nodded. "I agree. But, how?"

"I have no idea," Gerald said. "We could go through her garbage tonight and see what we can find on her. I think Sid's got some pictures of her sucking her thumb."

Arnold shook his head. "Naw . . . we should take the high road, Gerald."

Gerald blinked. "What high road?"

Arnold continued, "If she wants to run a dirty campaign, we should stay clean. The other kids are smart. They'll know the difference, and vote for us."

Gerald shook his head. "Smart? Arnold, have you met our classmates?"

Arnold and Gerald entered the classroom, passing Helga and Phoebe on their way to their desks. Again, Phoebe greeted Gerald with a tiny, guilty hello. This time, Gerald ignored it.

The morning passed slowly as Mr. Simmons lectured on about math, science, and social studies. But Arnold and Gerald couldn't concentrate. All they could think about was Helga. What did she know that they didn't? Maybe it was time to ask some fifth graders.

They found Wolfgang by the cafeteria door where he usually stood, giving random shoves to the third graders coming outside with their lunch trays.

"Helga? Yeah, I talked to her. What about it, tall-hair?" Wolfgang, the fifth-grade bully, towered over Gerald, who bravely squinted up at him.

"What's she got to do with a certain fifth-grade skateboard ramp?" Gerald asked.

Wolfgang snorted. "Why should I tell *you*?"

Arnold held out a bag of jelly beans. Wolfgang looked into the bag. "Watermelon?"

Arnold nodded. "Yeah, and peanut butter and coconut."

Wolfgang took the bag. "Okay. She stole your idea for a skateboard ramp. Then she got her dad to call up some construction guys he knows, and get them to pay for it." Wolfy snorted. "The ramp's prob'ly gonna have 'Big Bob's Beepers' painted all over it." He pointed to a corner of the playground. "It's goin' in right over there."

Arnold turned to Gerald in disbelief. "I can't believe Helga would go to so much trouble just to win."

Wolfgang laughed. "She hates you, man. She does it just to mess with your dumb football head. Anyways, like I care! Class president is for losers." He tripped a third grader. "Now stop buggin' me. I'm busy."

Arnold and Gerald walked off. "Nice talking to you, too, Wolfgang."

CHAPTER 8

While Arnold and Gerald talked outside, a worried Phoebe scribbled down notes as Helga took her coat out of her locker. "And bring plenty of tape, Phoebe. We'll put the new posters in the hall outside the cafeteria."

Phoebe checked her notes. She was getting tired of this. "I'm afraid that Rhonda already put up posters in that hallway."

Helga pulled her coat on. "No problem. We'll paper ours over Rhonda's."

Phoebe closed her notebook and cleared her throat. "Helga, I . . . don't feel right about the way our campaign is going. Your methods are . . . not exactly on the up-and-up."

Helga leaned into Phoebe's face. "Look, Phoebe. I want to be class president. And I don't care who I have to step on to get it, got it?"

Phoebe looked back at Helga, then tucked her notebook into her bag. "Fine," she said primly, and walked away.

Helga stared at Phoebe's back as she disappeared down the hall. "Phoebe? Where ya goin'? We gotta make posters! Phoebe!" The door closed at the end of the hallway. Helga muttered angrily as she slammed her locker shut.

The sun was setting as Helga trudged into her house. She found Big Bob watching the fights on TV. "Dad? Can I talk to you?"

Bob didn't turn from the screen. "Hit 'im with the left! The left! Oooh! That's gonna hurt tomorrow."

"Dad, you know that skateboard ramp for the fifth graders?"

Bob didn't look up. "You mean the one I'm payin' for?"

Helga nodded. "I was wondering if it's such a good idea."

That got his attention; Big Bob finally looked up. "Hey! Hey hey hey hey hey! What're you talkin' about? Last night you were beggin' me to do it. I've already called in a ton of favors to Nick and the guys at the Scheck Cement Company. They're all in. That skateboard ramp's as good as built. The ink's dry; that ship has sailed!" Big Bob turned back to his fight.

Helga trudged upstairs to her room. She

opened her closet door, parted her hangered clothes, knelt on the floor, and turned on the Christmas lights. Helga sighed a wistful sigh as she gazed at her Arnold Shrine. "Oh, my tender, foolish, right-minded little candidate. How I have betrayed thee! And yet I must continue to fight you to the bitter end."

She hung her head, barely able to face even the crude, handmade replica of the boy she loved. "I know that in the selfish pursuit of my goal, I may seem to be a scheming, cursed wretch, but please don't jump to conclusions. Things aren't always what they seem, my love!"

Helga reached out and touched Arnold's grassy cheek. "Dearest Arnold! Tomorrow we vote. Please forgive me this final day of mudslinging!" Helga closed her eyes and bowed her head.

CHAPTER 9

Finally the big day arrived. Mr. Simmons stood at the chalkboard. "Class! Today is the day we've all been waiting for: the democratic process in action! Election day! Now I know we're all eager to hear our candidates' final speeches, so let's get started. Rhonda?"

Rhonda walked primly to the podium. "Thank you. I care about this fourth-grade class. Over the past two weeks, I've listened to the concerns of my fellow students, and they have become my concerns. Like Sid, whose pet peeve is long cafeteria lines; and Stinky, who wonders how a simple country boy is going to be able to afford new art supplies."

Helga rolled her eyes and groaned out loud. "Somebody, toss her a cryin' towel!"

Rhonda glared at Helga, then continued. "In the last two weeks there has been plenty of mudslinging and dishonesty. I won't name any names, *Helga* and *Arnold*, but I feel that certain campaigns have made this whole democratic process thing . . . very unpleasant."

She pointed at the class. "*You* can change that. A vote for Rhonda Lloyd is a vote for decency and good taste. So remember: For a tasteful presidency, vote Rhonda. Thank you." She sat down as the class applauded.

Helga made a rude armpit noise and

grinned at Phoebe, who looked away uncomfortably.

Arnold was next at the podium. His gaze rested on Helga. She scowled back. Then Arnold began. "Well, Rhonda's right; it has been kind of a mean campaign. People have called other people names."

Helga scrunched down ever so slightly in her chair. Arnold looked right at her and continued. "The thing I want to say is . . . I may appear in some people's words to be a 'big, fat liar,' but please don't jump to conclusions. Things aren't always what they seem."

Helga grew hot; she felt her heart pierced with a flaming arrow of shame as her beloved repeated her secret thoughts of last night—almost word for word! She reeled in a haze of tormented feelings as Arnold finished his speech and sat down. She barely heard

Mr. Simmons call her name—it was her turn!

Helga took a deep breath, then staggered up to the front of the class as the kids hooted and clapped. She gripped the podium and calmed herself. "Okay, you morons, listen up. I . . . maybe spoke too soon about certain football heads being big, fat liars."

The class gasped. Was Helga G. Pataki actually making a *retraction*?

"I mean . . . maybe it wasn't my idea to build a fifth-grade skateboard ramp. Maybe it was Arnold's idea and I convinced my dad to pay for it. So maybe he didn't cheat or lie or steal an idea or anything."

Arnold's eyes widened. He smiled at her.

Helga gripped the podium tighter and resisted the urge to swoon or slap herself. She gritted her teeth, forcing herself to go on. "But . . . that doesn't mean that a skateboard ramp isn't a dumb idea! I mean, come on, how many of you clods actually own a skateboard?"

Several hands went up. Helga scowled and waved her arm dismissively. "Anyway, forget about skateboard ramps for a second! My point is this. I've still got the qualifications you want in a president: Leadership! Take-no-prisoners kind of leadership! A president that will fight for your rights in the classroom and in the hallways, so you can say it out loud: fourth grade and proud!" She pumped her fist in the air. "Vote Helga G. Pataki for president!"

The class was on their feet, roaring approval. Arnold, Gerald, Rhonda, and even Phoebe were clapping. As Helga walked back to her desk, she passed Mr. Simmons. Could that be a tear he was wiping away?

"Wonderful. Very moving, Ms. Pataki. And

now, our last speech before we vote is, of course—Curly!"

Curly sprang to the podium and nodded to his classmates. "Hello, fellow Martians. As you know, we have the entire lunch period to vote, so please drop by the little information booth that I've opened outside the cafeteria. And remember, vote for me, Curly 'My Dad Owns an Ice-cream Company' Gammelthorpe!"

The lunch bell rang, and Curly dashed out of the room. Mr. Simmons called out to the kids as they left their desks: "Remember, class. The ballot box is right here. Vote anytime during lunch period!"

CHAPTER 10

Arnold, Gerald, Rhonda, Nadine, Helga, and Phoebe went straight to Mr. Simmons's booth and cast their votes.

Meanwhile, Harold led the rest of the class out the door to see what Curly was talking about. Outside the cafeteria they gathered around a little card table with a simple, hand-lettered sign that read ASK ME ABOUT CURLY FOR PRESIDENT. Stinky walked away from Curly's table holding a coupon. He couldn't believe his eyes: "Willikers! Says here it's good for one free ice cream at Gammelthorpe's!"

Curly nodded, grinning. "That's right, Stinkeroo! And there're ten more where that came from if you vote for me!"

The others crowded in. "Me next! Me next!" they yelled.

After lunch, Mr. Simmons counted all the ballots. He reported the amazing news: Curly had won in a landslide! Arnold, Helga, and Rhonda all stared, dumbstruck.

Curly yelled, "I'm president! I'm president!" He jumped up on top of Mr. Simmons's desk, high-kicking and singing, "Tah-rah rah BOOM de-ayyy!" Then he ran out of the room, laughing. "So long, suckers!"

Mr. Simmons called after Curly as he disappeared down the hall. "Curly? It's only one-fifteen. Curly? Where are you going? Come back!"

At three o'clock the final bell rang. The kids poured out of P.S. 118 and down the street. Arnold watched Gerald walk off with Phoebe. He joked about something, and she laughed; it looked like they were friends again.

Arnold turned and saw Helga walking the other way up the sidewalk. "Helga?" he called out.

Helga scowled at Arnold as he ran to catch up with her. "Yeah? What do *you* want ?"

Arnold shrugged. "I don't know . . . I guess I wanted to thank you for what you said today. It took guts."

Helga was thrilled; she hid a secret little smile. Then she regained her composure, tough as ever. "Hey, why not? Who could beat Curly, anyway?"

Arnold laughed. "Yeah. The kid with the ice-cream store."

"Weird little freak," Helga added. "I tell ya, football head, it's a funny world. You may not be class president, but I talked to my dad, and it looks like you're still gonna get your skateboard ramp, courtesy of Scheck Cement, Vermicelli Towing, and Big Bob's Beepers."

Arnold grinned. "Really? That's great!" Arnold kicked a can. "You know what? I'm kinda glad Curly won. I've had enough of politics."

Helga nodded. "Me too." They reached the corner. "Until next year," she said. "And then I'm gonna kick your butt, football head."

about the author

Hey Arnold! creator Craig Bartlett was born in Seattle, Washington. He wanted to grow up to be either an artist or a secret agent, but became an animator instead. He moved to Los Angeles in 1987 to direct the Penny cartoons for *PeeWee's Playhouse.* Craig stayed to write and direct on the first season of *Rugrats,* which introduced him to his friends at Nickelodeon. He premiered his first episode of *Hey Arnold!* on Nick in 1996, and has since made 100 episodes. He lives with his wife, Lisa, and kids, Matt and Katie, in Glendale, California, and enjoys painting, snorkeling, and reading the *New Yorker* magazine, preferably in Hawaii.

YOU CAN ENTER FOR A CHANCE TO WIN A TRIP FOR FOUR TO NICKELODEON STUDIOS® FLORIDA!

1 GRAND PRIZE:
A 3-day/2-night trip for four to Nickelodeon Studios in Orlando, Florida

3 FIRST PRIZES:
A Sony Playstation® system and a *Rugrats™ in Paris* Playstation game from THQ®

25 SECOND PRIZES:
A *The Wild Thornberrys* CD-ROM from Mattel Interactive

100 THIRD PRIZES:
A set of four books from Simon & Schuster Children's Publishing, including a *The Wild Thornberrys* title, a *Rugrats* title, a *SpongeBob SquarePants* title, and a *Hey Arnold!* title

Complete entry form and send to:
Simon & Schuster Children's Publishing Division
Marketing Department/ "Nickelodeon Studios Florida Sweepstakes"
1230 Avenue of the Americas, 4th Floor, NY, NY 10020

Name_____ Birthdate___/___/_____

Address_____

City_____ State_____ Zip_____

Phone (____) _____

Parent/Guardian Signature _____

See back for official rules.

Simon & Schuster Children's Publishing Division/ "Nickelodeon Studios Florida Sweepstakes" Sponsor's Official Rules:

NO PURCHASE NECESSARY.

Enter by mailing this completed Official Entry Form (no copies allowed) or by mailing a 3 1/2" x 5" card with your complete name and address, parent and/or legal guardian's name, daytime telephone number, and birthdate to the Simon & Schuster Children's Publishing Division/ "Nickelodeon Studios Florida Sweepstakes," 1230 Avenue of the Americas, 4th Floor, NY, NY 10020. Entry forms are available in the back of *The Rugrats Files #3: The Quest for the Holey Pail* (12/2000*), Rugrats Chapter Book #10: Dil in a Pickle* (11/2000*), The Wild Thornberrys Chapter Book #2: Two Promises Too Many!* (9/2000), *The Wild Thornberrys Chapter Book #3: A Time to Share* (9/2000), *SpongeBob SquarePants Trivia Book* (9/2000), *SpongeBob SquarePants Joke Book* (9/2000), *Hey Arnold! Chapter Book #1: Arnold for President* (9/2000), and *Hey Arnold! Chapter Book #2: Return of the Sewer King* (9/2000), and on the web site SimonSaysKids.com. Sweepstakes begins 8/1/2000 and ends 2/28/2001. Entries must be postmarked by 2/28/01 and received by 3/15/01. Not responsible for lost, late, damaged, postage-due, stolen, illegible, mutilated, incomplete, or misdirected or not delivered entries or mail, or for typographical errors in the entry form or rules. Entries are void if they are in whole or in part illegible, incomplete, or damaged. Enter as often as you wish, but each entry must be mailed separately. Entries will not be returned. Winners will be selected at random from all eligible entries received in a drawing to be held on or about 3/30/01. Grand prize winner must be available to travel during the months of June and July 2001. If Grand Prize winner is unable to travel on the specified dates, prize will be forfeited and awarded to an alternate. Winners will be notified by mail within 30 days of selection. The grand prize winner will be notified by phone as well. Odds of winning depend on the number of eligible entries received.

Prizes: One Grand Prize: A 3-day/2-night trip for four to Nickelodeon Studios in Orlando, FL, including a VIP tour, admission for four to Universal Studios Florida, round-trip coach airfare from a major U.S. airport nearest the winner's residence, and standard hotel accommodations (2 rooms, double occupancy) of sponsor's choice. (Total approx. retail value: $2,700.00). Winner must be accompanied by a parent or legal guardian. Prize does not include transfers, gratuities, or any other expenses not specified or listed herein. 3 First Prizes: A Sony Playstation system and a *Rugrats* Playstation game from THQ. (Total approx. retail value: $150.00 each). 25 Second Prizes: A *The Wild Thornberrys* CD-ROM from Mattel Interactive. (Approx. retail value: $29.99 each). 100 Third Prizes: A set of four books from Simon & Schuster Children's Publishing, including a *The Wild Thornberrys* title, a *Rugrats* title, a *SpongeBob SquarePants* title, and a *Hey Arnold!* title. (Total approx. retail value: $12.00 per set).

The sweepstakes is open to legal residents of the continental U.S. (excluding Puerto Rico) and Canada (excluding Quebec) ages 5-13 as of 2/28/01. Proof of age is required to claim prize. Prizes will be awarded to winner's parent or legal guardian. Void wherever prohibited or restricted by law. All provincial, federal, state, and local laws apply. Simon & Schuster Inc. and MTV Networks and their respective officers, directors, shareholders, employees, suppliers, parent companies, subsidiaries, affiliates, agencies, sponsors, participating retailers, and persons connected with the use, marketing, or conducting of this sweepstakes are not eligible. Family members living in the same household as any of the individuals referred to in the preceding sentence are not eligible.

One prize per person or household. Prizes are not transferable, have no cash equivalent, and may not be substituted except by sponsors, in the event of prize unavailability, in which case a prize of equal or greater value will be awarded. All prizes will be awarded.

If a winner is a Canadian resident, then he/she must correctly answer a skill-based question administered by mail.

All expenses on receipt and use of prize including provincial, federal, state, and local taxes are the sole responsibility of the winner's parent or legal guardian. Winners' parents or legal guardians may be required to execute and return an Affidavit of Eligibility and Publicity Release and all other legal documents which the sweepstakes sponsors may require (including a W-9 tax form) within 15 days of attempted notification or an alternate winner will be selected. The grand prize winner, parent or legal guardian, and travel companions will be required to execute a liability release form prior to ticketing.

Winners' parents or legal guardians on behalf of the winners agree to allow use of winners' names, photographs, likenesses, and entries for any advertising, promotion, and publicity purposes without further compensation to or permission from the entrants, except where prohibited by law.

Winners and winners' parents or legal guardians agree that Simon & Schuster, Inc., Nickelodeon Studios, THQ, and MTV Networks and their respective officers, directors, shareholders, employees, suppliers, parent companies, subsidiaries, affiliates, agencies, sponsors, participating retailers, and persons connected with the use, marketing, or conducting of this sweepstakes shall have no responsibility or liability for injuries, losses, or damages of any kind in connection with the collection, acceptance, or use of the prizes awarded herein, or from participation in this promotion.

By participating in this sweepstakes, entrants agree to be bound by these rules and the decisions of the judges and sweepstakes sponsors, which are final in all matters relating to the sweepstakes. Failure to comply with the Official Rules may result in a disqualification of your entry and further participation in this sweepstakes.

The first names of the winners will be posted at SimonSaysKids.com or the first names of the winners may be obtained by sending a stamped, self-addressed envelope after 3/30/01 to Prize Winners, Simon & Schuster Children's Publishing Division "Nickelodeon Studios Sweepstakes," 1230 Avenue of the Americas, 4th Floor, NY, NY 10020.

Sponsor of sweepstakes is Simon & Schuster Inc.